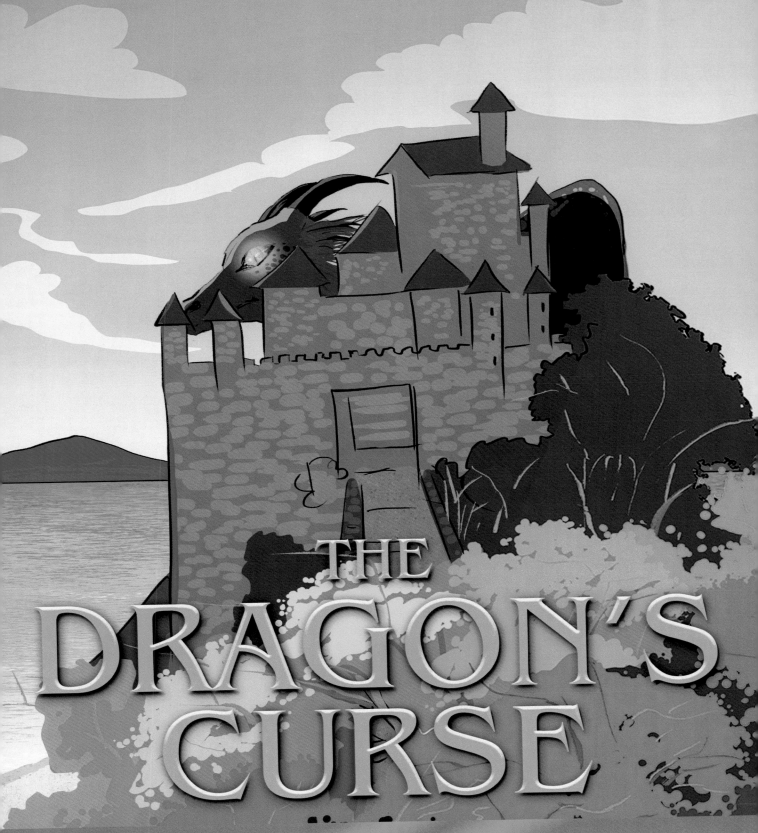

THE DRAGON'S CURSE

LUCY BLAIR

Print information available on the last page

Rev. date: 05/16/2019

To order additional copies of this book, contact:
Xlibris
1-888-795-4274
www.Xlibris.com
Orders@Xlibris.com

THE
DRAGON'S
CURSE

Once upon a time, there was a queen. She was a beautiful queen that walked in grace and elegance. But her beauty was deceiving, for she was vain, full of greed, and cold-hearted. The only love she had in her heart, was for treasure. The queen had the finest of treasure taken for her.

Ships full of diamonds, emeralds, gold, and opals. Wagons carrying silver, rubies, and pearls. She even went so far as to send out her soldiers to raid villages, and plunder them of their prized goods. Indeed, she cared for nothing and no one, other than her precious treasure.

One evening, an angry dragon smashed down the walls of the queen's castle, for he was outraged that the queen's soldiers had stolen his treasure. The dragon looked around to see all the treasure the queen had, overfilled and spilling out of large rooms. "Arrogant fool!" The dragon boomed "Has your lust for treasure blinded you so? That you would dare steal from a dragon!"

The dragon saw that the queen cared not if he burnt down her kingdom. He saw that she had not a single drop of kindness in her heart. "Vain and greedy of heart" he said "Queen of murderous beauty and punished treasure. If you love your treasure so much, then you may keep it!"

The queen was then suddenly engulfed in the dragon's magical blue fire, making the tips of her toes turn into diamond. If the queen could not find true love and kindness within herself, and push away her greed for treasure, then she would turn into the jewels she loved so, forever joining them in their lifeless beauty.

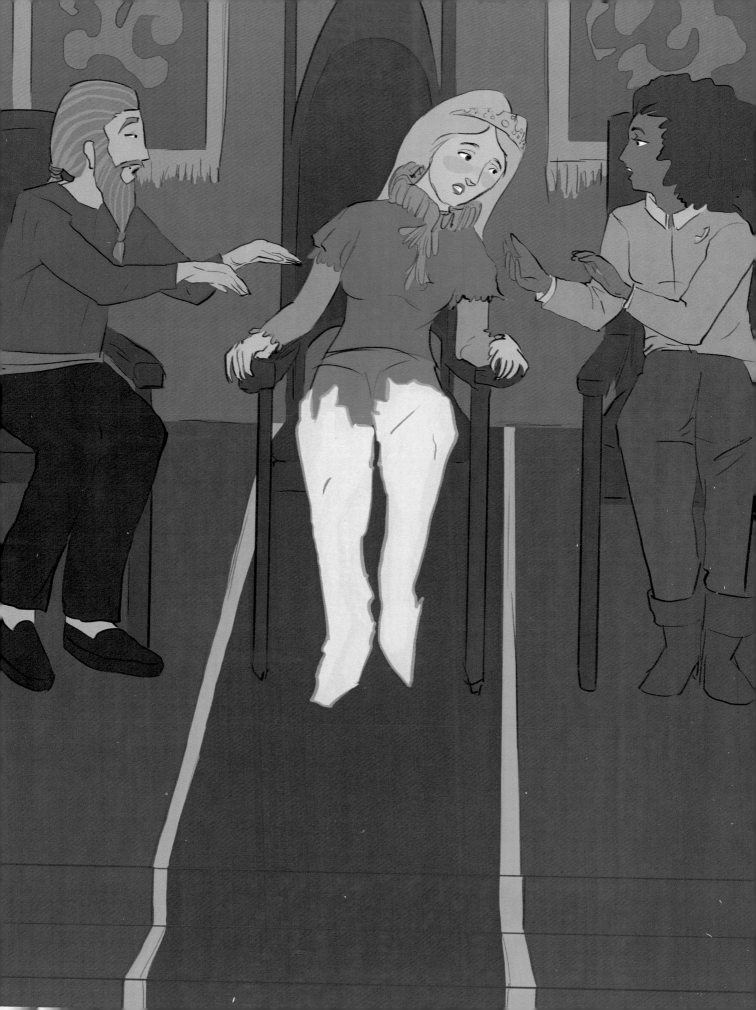

The queen summoned her royal advisors for answers to the dragon's curse, for each day that passed, the more her body hardened into diamond. "Simply cut off your feet, my queen!" an advisor suggested "It will stop the curse from spreading, and you may keep your treasure!" Not wanting to cut off her feet, the queen sent her advisors away and began to weep in despair and fear of the dragon's curse.

As time passed, the queen struggled to walk as her legs were now solid diamond "Perhaps a ride around the kingdom will lift your spirits" a servant suggested. So the queen got into her carriage and rode throughout her kingdom. The queen saw how poor her people were, dirty and hungry for food. The queen began to feel pity in her heart for them.

It was not long before the queen's hands and torso were turned entirely into diamond. The queen wept into her diamond hands, crying out "I can no longer feel anything! Not even my own tears!" The queen fell into despair as she lost hope of ever returning to normal. She could not help herself, but she could help others. The queen thought back and remembered the people of her kingdom. The growth of the queen's diamond body had finally reached her neck when she called her advisors to her "If I shall perish, then it will be in the interest of my kingdom" she said.

"Once my transformation is complete and I am no more, you must shatter my body to pieces and give them to the poor, so that they may eat and sleep with ease". Once these words left the queen's mouth, she had completely turned into diamond. Following the queen's wish, the advisors gathered the servants and gave them mallets to smash and shatter the queen's body.

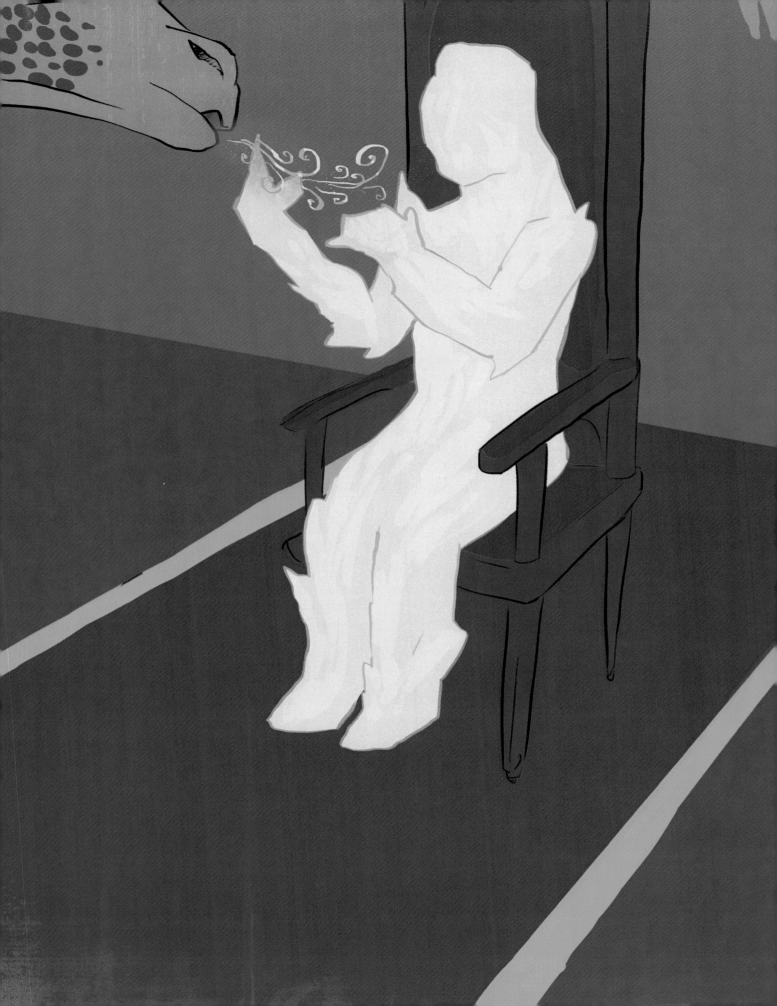

They surrounded the diamond statue that was once their queen and raised their weapons "Stop!" A voice thundered. The dragon had returned. The dragon furled his large wings and approached the queen's statue, his burning eyes examining her. The dragon suddenly blew out his fire at the queen's statue, and all of the servants and advisors watched in awe and wonderment.

They watched in amazement as the diamond began melting off the queen, freeing her from her jeweled prison. The queen looked up at the dragon and asked why he had spared her "I did not spare you" he answered "Your own heart has! By letting kindness enter it and allowing love to reside in it" he said.

"By your willing sacrifice to offer your punishment as a gift to your people, you have shown both love and kindness". The queen wept tears of joy and gave the dragon's treasure back to him, along with the stolen treasures to their due villages. Whatever treasure was left, the queen gave to her people, vowing to forever give them a happy and prosperous life as their benevolent queen.

THE END

Printed in the United States
By Bookmasters